P9-DGU-862

APR 2001

Knock at the Door

AND OTHER BABY ACTION RHYMES

KAY CHORAO

DUTTON CHILDREN'S BOOKS • NEW YORK

NORTHPORT PUBLIC LIBRARY
NORTHPORT, NEW YORK

Copyright © 1999 by Kay Sproat Chorao
All rights reserved.

CIP Data is available.

Published in the United States 1999 by Dutton Children's Books,
a division of Penguin Putnam Books for Young Readers
345 Hudson Street, New York, New York 10014
http://www.penguinputnam.com/yreaders/index.htm

Designed by Sara Reynolds
Printed in Hong Kong
First Edition
ISBN 0-525-45969-3
3 5 7 9 10 8 6 4

Contents

Pink and Pearl
MARKET

This Little Piggy

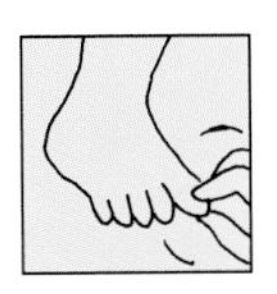

This little piggy went to market,

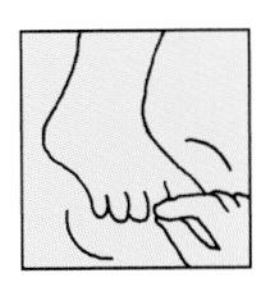

This little piggy stayed home,

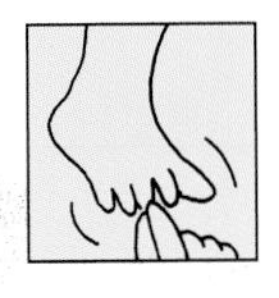

This little piggy had roast beef,

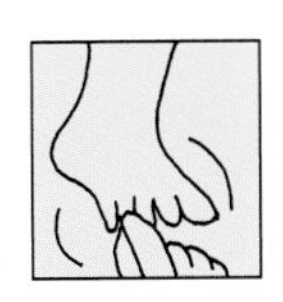

This little piggy had none,

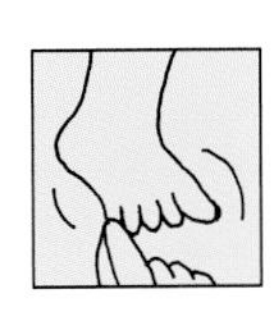

This little piggy cried, "Wee, wee, wee"
All the way home!

Five Little Sparrows

Five little sparrows
High in a tree.

The first one says,
"What DO I see?"

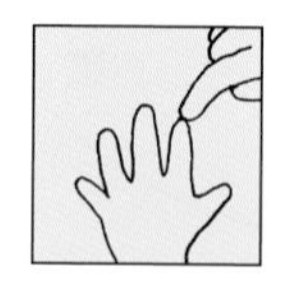

The second one says,
"I see the street."

The third one says,
"And SEEDS to eat."

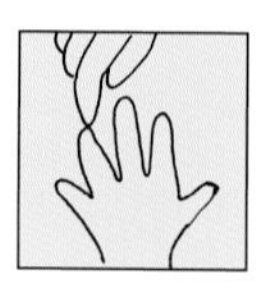

The fourth one says,
"The seeds are WHEAT."

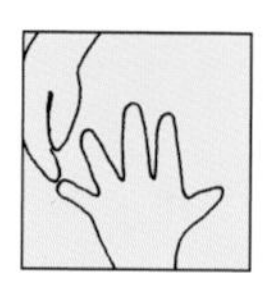

The fifth one says,
"Tweet, tweet."

Horsey, Horsey

Horsey, horsey, ride with me
Across the land, across the sea.
Horsey, horsey, ride with me,

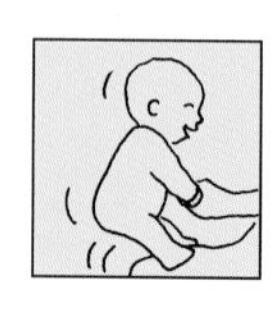

But DO NOT LET ME

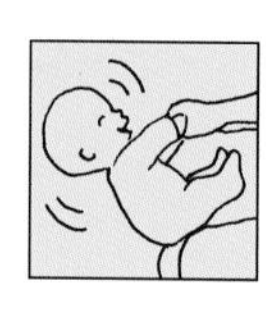

F—A—L—L.

Giddyap, Horsey

Giddyap, horsey, to the fair.
What'll we buy when we get there?
A penny apple and a penny pear.
Giddyap, horsey, to the fair.

Choo-choo Train

This is a choo-choo train,
Puffing down the track.
Now it's going forward,
Now it's going back.

Now the bell is ringing,

Now the whistle blows.

What a lot of noise it makes
Everywhere it goes.

Kitten Is Hiding

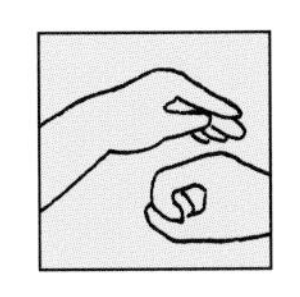

A kitten is hiding under a chair.

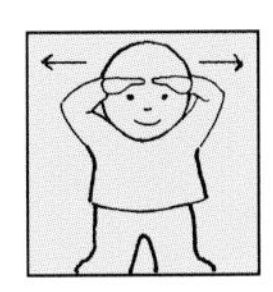

I looked and I looked for her everywhere.

Under the table and under the bed;
I looked in the corner, and when I said,

"Come, kitty, come, kitty, here's milk for you,"

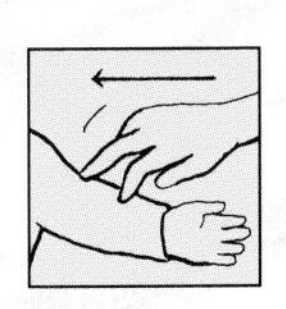

Kitty came running and calling, "Mew, mew."

Knock at the Door

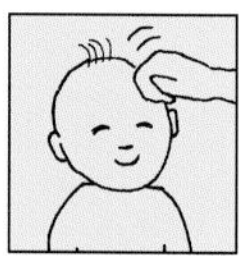

Knock at the door,

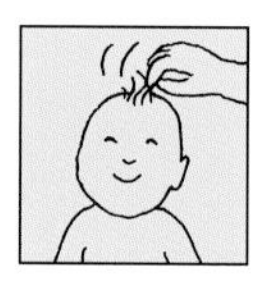

Pull the bell,

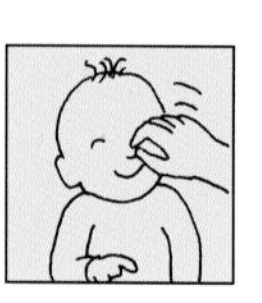

Lift the latch,

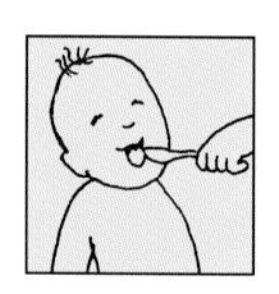

And walk right in!

Carrots

Five Little Ducks

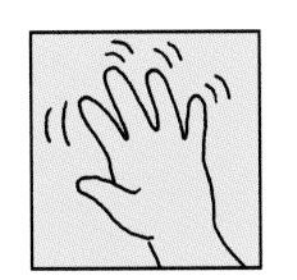

Five little ducks went in for a swim;

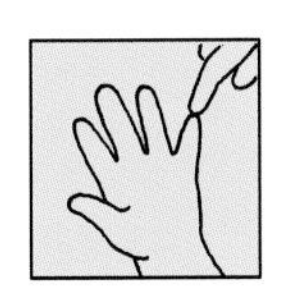

The first little duck put his head in.

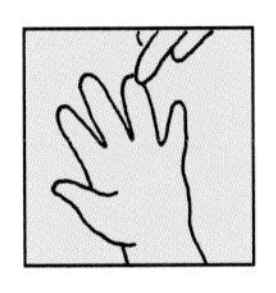

The second little duck put his head back;

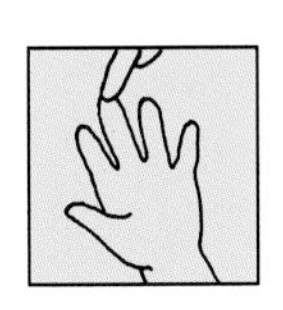

The third little duck said, “Quack, quack, quack.”

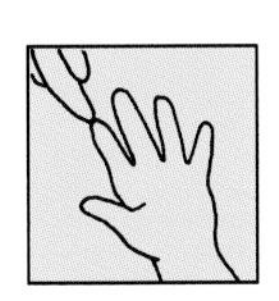

The fourth little duck with his tiny brother

Went for a walk with his father and mother.

Pat-a-Cake

Pat-a-cake, pat-a-cake,
Baker's man,
Bake me a cake as fast as you can.

Pat it

And poke it

And mark it with a B,

And toss it in the oven
For Baby and me.

Hot Cross Buns

Hot cross buns,
Hot cross buns,

One-a-penny, two-a-penny,

Hot cross buns.

Little Mousie

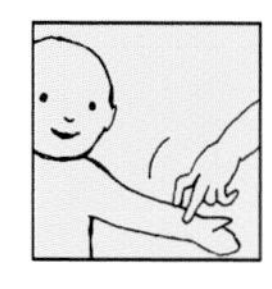

See the little mousie

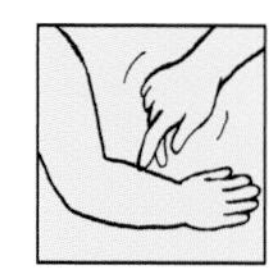

Creeping up the stair,
Looking for a warm nest.

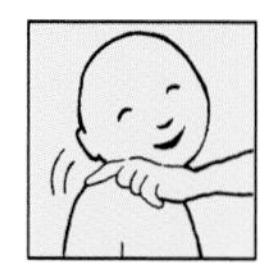

There—oh! there.

Baby Mice

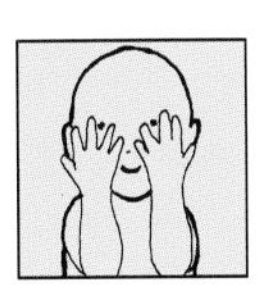

Where are the big mice? Squeak, squeak, squeak.

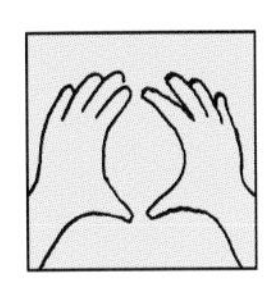

I cannot see them. Peek, peek, peek.

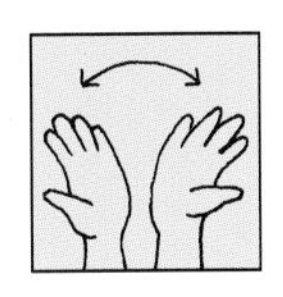

Here they come from the hole in the wall,

One, two, three, four, five—that's all!

Once I Saw a Bunny

Once I saw a bunny

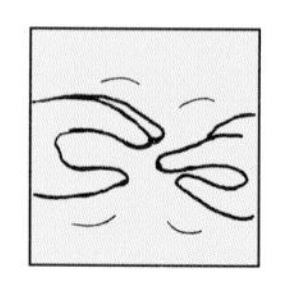

And a green cabbage head.
"I think I'll have some cabbage,"
The little bunny said.

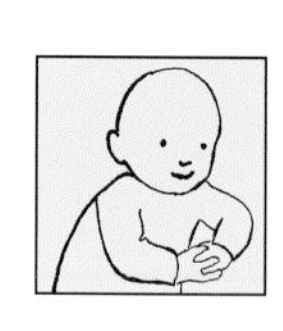

So he nibbled and he nibbled.
And he pricked his ears to say,

"Now I think it's time
I should be hopping on my way."

Slowly, Slowly

Slowly, slowly, very slowly
Creeps the garden snail;

Slowly, slowly, very slowly

Up the wooden rail.

MOUSE

Round and Round

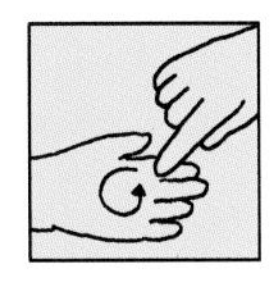

Round and round the garden
Went the teddy bear;

One step,
Two steps,

Tickly under there.

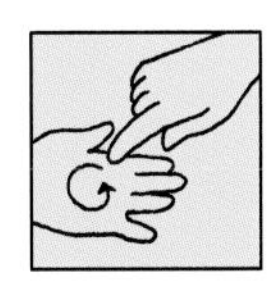

Round and round the haystack
Went the little mouse;

One step,
Two steps,

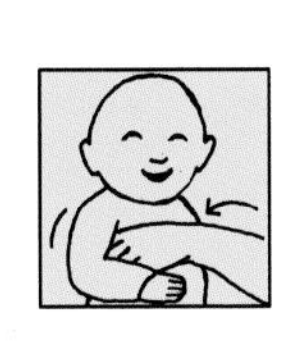

In his little house.

The Teapot

I'm a little teapot, short and stout.

This is my handle,

This is my spout.

When I get all steamed up, then I shout.
Just tip me over and pour me out.

Peas Porridge

Peas porridge hot,
Peas porridge cold,
Peas porridge in the pot,
Nine days old.
Some like it hot,
Some like it cold,
Some like it in the pot
Nine days old.

Here's a Ball for Baby

Here's a ball for baby,
Big and soft and round.

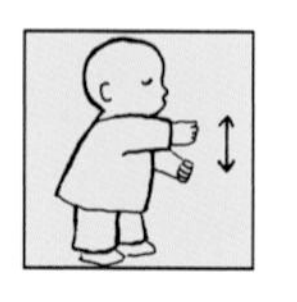

Here's the baby's hammer—
See how she can pound.

Here's the baby's music,
Clapping, clapping so.

Here's the baby's foot,
Tapping, tapping so.
Here's the baby's trumpet,
Toot, toot, toot, toot, too.
Here's the way the baby
Plays at peekaboo.
Here's a big umbrella
To keep the baby dry.
And here's the baby's cradle,
Rock-a-baby-bye.

Bunnies' Bedtime

"My bunnies now must go to bed,"
The little mother rabbit said.

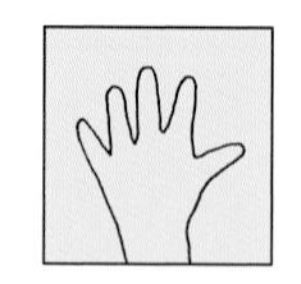

"But I will count them first to see
If they have all come back to me.

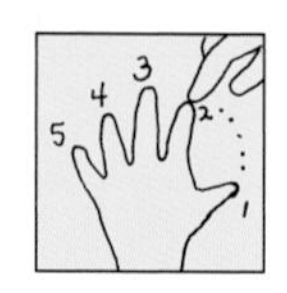

One bunny, two bunnies, three bunnies dear,
Four bunnies, five bunnies—yes, all are here.

They are the prettiest things alive—

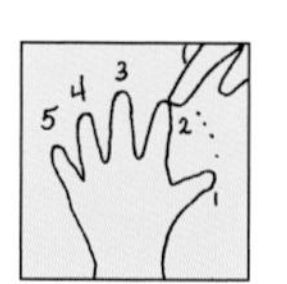

My bunnies, one, two, three, four, five."

Doggie's Tail
A little doggie, all brown and black,
Wore his tail curled on his back.